Katie Piper

ALL YOU NEED

Illustrated by Tilia Rand-Bell

This is a mouse,
but not just any mouse.
This is Teeny Mouse.

And Teeny Mouse is going
on a big adventure –

a journey she's never taken before.

And though it's BIG,
and FUN,
and EXCITING

... she suddenly feels a little bit small.

Don't worry, Teeny Mouse.
All you need is a little bit of...

So Teeny Mouse moves forward, further into the forest, until lots of leaves make the light disappear.

And because it's **DARK,**

and **COLD,**

and **SCARY**

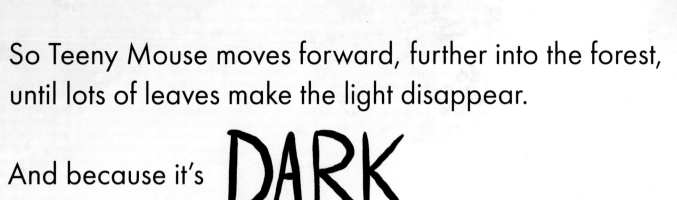

KEEP GOING

GO BACK

...she suddenly feels a little bit lost.

Don't worry Teeny Mouse.
All you need is a little bit of courage
and a little bit of...

So Teeny Mouse goes on, as the sun rises higher,
until her teeny tummy starts to stir.

And because the way is LONG,

and it's LATE,

and it's LUNCHTIME

...she suddenly feels a little bit hungry.

Don't worry, Teeny Mouse.

All you need is a little bit of COURAGE,

a little bit of FAITH,

and a little bit of...

KINDNESS!

So Teeny Mouse goes on,
just a little bit longer,
until she stumbles upon a
meadow full of fruit.

But because it's huge,

and goes on,

and on

. . . she suddenly feels a little bit tired.

Don't worry, Teeny Mouse.

All you need is a little bit of COURAGE,
a little bit of FAITH,

a little bit of **KINDNESS,**

and a little bit of…

So Teeny Mouse heads home,
as the moon and stars appear,
back through the
meadow of fruit,
the forest
and field.

And because it's been BIG,

and FUN, and EXCITING

...she suddenly feels
like it's a little too much.

Don't worry, Teeny Mouse.

All you need is a little bit of COURAGE,
a little bit of FAITH,

a little bit of **KINDNESS,**
a little bit of **JOY,**

and a little bit of...

CALM. (Shhhh!)